I0456935

# The Lost Kingdom

## A Legends of the Five Crowns Novella

### MISTY EVANS & MICHELLE MILES

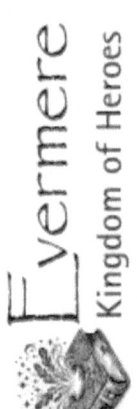

Seabright
Haven

Seabright
Kingdom of the seas

Brightwater

Tidewatch

Evermere
Kingdom of Heroes

Thornveil
Kingdom of Shadows

Fablehollow

Fairton

Longmere

Drakenholt
Kingdom of Beasts

Aurelia
Kingdom of Light

Fairy tales always begin with *Once Upon a Time*.
Quests begin with *Once Upon a Calling*...

# CHAPTER ONE

## DESSALYN | THE DREAM

THE SKY BLEEDS COPPER, thick and viscous as if the sun itself has been wounded.

I walk through the bones of a kingdom I don't recognize, though my feet seem to know every crack in the once polished marble floor. Empty towers stand like the ribs of a beast half-buried in ash. The hot air stinks of wet earth, dragon smoke, and the metallic tang of endings. A battle that's been lost.

A familiar sensation sits in my stomach. For some reason, I'm sure I've walked this path before. Regardless of my gut, my mind tells a different story. *I'm not supposed to be here.*

I keep walking.

My boots crunch over shattered tiles that once made a mosaic of five crowns—four still glisten gold under the dust. The fifth is cracked straight through, the color leeched from it.

Wind howls through the arches above me. I hear a voice calling my name in a language I shouldn't understand.

"*Dessalyn. My storykeeper.*"

Not a whisper. Not a plea. A command.

My heart stumbles, my mouth goes dry. *Run*, my brain commands.

My feet stay planted. The floor under me, the crumbling walls around me, the bleak sky above...it *needs* me. I will not leave it.

So I stand my ground and turn.

A shimmer of magic ripples out from me. I'm a disturbance in this place, a rock dropped into standing water. The air coils around my throat—wet, hot, and choking. My vision blurs, then clears, revealing a new scene.

At the far end of a ruined hall, a figure sits on a half-crumbled throne. He's draped in royal crimson, the fabric stained and edged with soot. Long, dark blond hair brushes his broad shoulders and covers his face as he rests his forehead in his hands. Thick, gold bracelets glint around his wrists, but they're as cracked as the stones. The crown on his head glints like dragonbone.

My breath catches. Something in my chest reacts—like a string pulled tight.

The crown. The throne. His cape.

A prince?

*Drakenholt.* The name echoes in my head, creating a new ripple. One of the five kingdoms of Edeia, Drakenholt's legends are whispered about in fireside tales and warnings, where shapeshifters, dragons, and wild, ancient magic rule.

The stuff of fairy tales. Stories that I'm quite familiar with. I write and translate them every day to keep the realm running smoothly. But this...This is no happy ending.

A new thought tickles the edges of my mind. *Is this my quest?* To find something or someone in this kingdom? To save them?

Too late for that, if this dream is any indication.

Sadness blooms in my chest. I'm always too late. *Just like I was with Mom.*

At twenty-four, I still haven't received my fated quest from the sentient book of Lore. As a citizen of Evermere, the Kingdom of Heroes, I am destined to receive a quest that will change my life. My calling will come with a noble warrior. A valuable sidekick. Trials and obstacles, but also courage, skills, and resourcefulness to overcome them. A happy ending.

Not this—a burned-out, ruined kingdom. A dying story.

Since Mom's death, I've experienced nothing but death, destruction, and twisted tales.

Perhaps this *is* where I'm meant to be, but even so, what if I'm not ready? Worse, what if no story will ever choose me at all? What if I'm not meant to have a happy ending?

The fear haunts me more than I care to admit. I'm not good enough. Not brave enough. Not meant to be a heroine. I'm just a Lorewyn without a quest, fated to watch others finish their stories while mine never begins.

A strangled sound comes from the figure on the throne, sending feverish shivers down my spine. My memory pushes a new thought to the surface.

*The crown prince of Drakenholt.*

I rub my temple where the words press against it. If that's true, shouldn't I know him?

I've read tales about a prince who breathes life into stories. Legends that claim he speaks and tales come to life. That his stories can heal a broken heart. Grant a dying wish.

He's not so different from my sister and me, the lorekeepers of Evermere. Our business, our mission, is to save and share the realm's stories. Is that his mission as well?

I scan the destruction of the palace around him. Destroyed pillars. Giant tree roots that have cleaved through the floors. Broken stained-glass windows. Smoke and ash, hanging in the air.

Did *he* do this? Did he destroy his castle and throne?

Why?

Where is his family? The courtiers? The citizens of this place? Did he...murder them?

Another sound slips from his mouth, raw and ragged. But it's not the sound of a man. It's feral, deep, wild. The sound a caged monster might make. Rage rides it, and his shoulders shake with a kind of savagery that claws at my ribcage and makes my already uneven breathing falter.

Instinct yells at me again to *run*. To fear the man, the monster on his wrecked throne.

*It's only a dream*, my logical brain tells me, trying to override my instincts. My emotions join it. His anger is underlaid by sadness. A sadness that causes an ache in my chest. He's grieving a loss.

My own grief responds, pulling me closer.

For now, I'm convinced this is a quest. *My* quest. I don't know where it's leading me, but as with all quests, the journey must always move forward. There is no turning back.

The heat intensifies, and the ash thickens, cloying and bitter on my tongue. My breath gasps in and out of my lungs, and the ripples caused by the movement spread to him. Engulf him.

He tenses, his head lifting a fraction. Something dark dangles from a chain around his neck. An obsidian pendant. On it is an engraved sigil, cracked through the center. I can't make out the design, yet I'm certain I've seen it before.

The urge to understand it forces me to take another step. My fingertips itch to touch it. I know so little about Drakenholt and its history. How does it fit with his story?

With mine?

Knowledge always came with a cost. Am I willing to pay it? "Who are you?" I whisper.

His head lifts slowly, the outline of green scales shimmering on his neck.

I suck in a breath at the sight, and my entire body recoils.

Eyes like wildfire lock on mine, and I tremble, realizing the flames reflected inside them can burn.

Then, everything goes white.

I wake up choking.

My fist grips the cotton blanket so hard my knuckles protest. The room is gray, the sun not yet fully risen. I blink into the shadows and try to remember where I am. *Who* I am.

Outside my open window, a rooster announces the dawn. Sparrows chirp. The scents of morning dew, ink, and lamp oil tangle in the air. *I'm in the cottage. I'm home.*

It was only a dream. I'm not the heroine of a story, and it was no quest. I'm just boring, responsible Dessalyn Lorewyn, awake at dawn to face another day in Fablehollow.

I push strands of hair from my eyes and force myself to sit up. Sweat beads at the back of my neck, and my sleeping gown clings to my damp skin. I toss back the sheet, only to find it tangled with my legs. Fighting it off, I swing around and press my bare feet to the stone floor.

My room is small but stubbornly mine, tucked between the scriptorium and the crooked chimney wall of our cottage. The ceiling slopes low over my bed, patched where my father once stopped a leak with story parchment. The parchment is still there, warped and stained, but holding.

A built-in bookshelf along the far wall is brimming with half-translated manuscripts, dog-eared fables, and my journals. I'm not sure why I write in them, detailing one boring day after another, but sometimes, it feels as if I'm tracking time with the entries.

Especially since Mom died. If I don't log the days, they blur into one. A part of me wants to believe that she's reading them as I write, keeping an eye on me and Calliope, my sister, from her place in the Fade.

A pair of garden boots, striped with mud, sit neatly at the edge of the rug. The rug itself—faded blue and frayed on one end—was a gift from Calliope, who claims it once belonged to a desert prince. I'm not sure if that's true, but I love the romantic sound of it. I love to pretend it has traveled far and that one day, the prince will show up here, looking for it. He'll fall madly in love with me and whisk me away to his desert castle.

Pure fiction, that is. Even if such a prince did appear on the doorstep, would I leave Fablehollow and what's left of my family? My insides are at war over that idea, but how can I have a grand adventure if I never leave home?

I rise, clean up in my tiny washroom, and pull on a clean moss-green dress. The fabric is worn but buttery soft. My mother's pendant hangs around my neck, and I rub it, her presence ghost-like in the aftermath of the dream, whose edges are already fading.

I've had them since I was a babe, and they often feel more like nightmares. She always comforted me after them, and although I'm no longer a child, I still long for her guidance.

Of her two daughters, I'm blessed—or cursed, depending on how you look at it—with her visions and prophecies. Sometimes they come to me in dreams; other times, when I'm fully awake. They are never subtle nor straightforward, and I'm not gifted at deciphering them. Not like she was.

*I wish you were here, Mom. Stars, I miss you.*

I snatch a journal from the highest shelf and scribble down what I can still remember of the dream. Even as I write, I feel more of it trying to slip away, the words struggling to come forth from my quill. No matter how I try to recreate the images in my head, I can't seem to do them justice in writing.

The band on my braid came loose during the night, so I set the journal aside to attend to it. On a stool in front of a cobbled together dresser with a cracked mirror, I run my fingers through the tangles. My reflection stares back at me, split in the middle.

The comb and brush on the dresser do little good with the snarls. Another thing I miss—my mother's ability to brush out my hair and make it cooperate. My fingers catch on a particularly intricate knot, and my mind flashes back to the twisted and chaotic throne room.

*The prince of...* The name of the kingdom teases the fringe of my memory. What was the name again?

I close my eyes to recall the details better. The smoke and ash. The crumbling throne. The look in the prince's eyes when he lifted his head.

*Drakenholt.*

That's it. I whisper the name aloud, but it feels odd on my tongue, as if I'm rolling marbles around on it. Why does it seem so familiar when I can't recall such a place?

I itch to search our library, but as the rooster crows right outside the window, reminding me of the time, I decide it will have to wait. There is much to be done before we open the shop.

I give up on the knot. Calliope will have to help me with it later. I hastily reweave my uncooperative locks, tie a ribbon around the braid's end, and grab my boots.

The floorboards creak under my steps as I leave my room, careful not to wake my sister. Her door is open enough to reveal a tangle of quilts and curls. A soft snore drifts out—delicate and defiant, as if she's making a point even in her sleep.

Although Calliope doesn't have Mom's gift, she always claims that dreams are where the real work happens. That we plow our subconscious like we till our garden, digging deep, cultivating and processing emotions, and mulching those no longer needed. I wonder if that's true, and what it might mean that I'm dreaming of a dying kingdom.

A shiver passes over me. Was it simply a dream, or a vision of the future? Is it possible Drakenholt is going to fall?

An odd question, since I'm not sure it even exists.

My gaze snags on the hall mirror beside Calliope's door as images come to life in its reflective surface. A grand ballroom filled with men and women in dazzling gowns and formal dinner wear, twirling to music. The ruined throne in perfect shape, with an older man sitting on it, his regal wife next to him, and a baby on her lap. Their older son, a handsome but arrogant prince, smirking behind a goblet of wine...

*The crown prince. I know him.*

Before I can focus on him, I see my mother, standing proud in a simple dress the color of sunflowers. She's addressing the king.

My heart clenches, my entire body going rigid. My voice comes out soft. "Mom?"

The moment it leaves my mouth, she turns her head to look at me. Our eyes meet, but too late. She and the scene vanish in a swirl of smoke.

For a long moment, I stare at my reflection but see her face instead. It blurs at the edges. Her eyes fade. Her mouth becomes washed out.

*No, no, no.*

I'm forgetting my mother's face.

Her likeness disappears entirely. All that remains is me with a giant crack through the mirror's surface. I reach up to run a finger along it. Did that just happen? I know it wasn't there yesterday.

I heave a guilty sigh. Must every mirror I stare into reward me by breaking?

Calliope's cat, Marsh, skirts past my ankles, startling me. He jets into her room, all long, dark hair and poofed tail.

Shaking off the vision, I take a few deep breaths to calm my heart. I pad to the scriptorium, where the door is invisible to all but us Lorewyns, and only those of our bloodline can enter. When I hold out my hand, the knob appears, and I crack it open to make sure all is well.

The scent of ink fills the room, sharp and comforting. Along with it, I catch a whiff of jasmine, and my heart aches as it always does when I smell my mother's perfume. It clings to the parchment and furniture as if she were in here all night, working away.

Candle stubs line the writing table and desks, half-melted into the trays we keep forgetting to replace. Someone left an uncorked bottle of violet ink open on one of the desks. Probably me. The magical liquid hums softly, a song ready to record the next story.

Next to it lies our mother's heirloom quill. A purely Fae device with a soul all its own, it refuses to write falsehoods and glows in the presence of corrupted text.

Lining the walls, the volumes on the sacred scriptorium shelves beckon to me. A rabbit hole that I can get sucked into for hours, days. Vellicor, the sentient book of Lore, rests in its cradle, slumbering like my family. Bulin, the owl who guards it, watches me with his dark, detached eyes. Another purely Fae creature, he never eats or sleeps. His only purpose is to safeguard the book.

While Vellicor lies silent, I swear I can feel it eager to spring to life. Could it finally be willing to reveal my quest? I'm nothing if not stubborn, and I wait long seconds, my skin prickling with anticipation.

But Vellicor does not wake, does not open.

*Not today.* I release a sigh, a mix of relief and disappointment. Yet, in my heart, I refuse to give up hope.

I close the door quietly and move on.

At the end of the hall, the mercantile stretches wide and crooked, all warm wood and mismatched shelves. The growing dawn light seeps through the stained-glass transoms, spilling soft color across the floor—blue, amber, green. My mind flashes back to the prince and his ruined throne room. I rub my chest where a new ache, this one yearning to go to him, mingles with my grief. I want to help him, but how?

*It was just a dream*, I tell myself. If such a prince exists, he's probably waking up to his lover after a night of debauchery. Someone will bring him breakfast, draw him a bath, pick out his clothes.

How different his life is from mine.

Father is asleep again in his chair in our tiny living room. His boots are off and scattered on the threadbare rug. One hand lies

MISTY EVANS & MICHELLE MILES

tucked under his chin. His spectacles are perched on the bridge of his nose, and an open volume rests on his chest. Something old and thick, the fraying thread whispering of neglect. I make a mental note to mend it later.

He hates it when his neck locks up after sleeping in this position, but something about the quiet, the early hour, the way his breathing rises and falls—I don't want to break it by waking him. He spends most nights since Mom died pacing the back porch, the garden, the woods. It's good that he succumbed to sleep last night.

I glance back toward the scriptorium door. He claims stories find us when we're still enough to listen. Something definitely found me last night.

I must feed the animals and make breakfast. Then it's a full day running the shop. But tonight...tonight I'll end up in the fabled library to write and rewrite, to translate and fix bindings.

And I'll search for legends about a prince who's part monster and waits in ash and agony.

# CHAPTER TWO

## DESSALYN

THE MORNING HUMIDITY ADDS another layer to my skin as I step into the back garden. Dew clings to the grass, silvering the path that winds past the herb beds and toward the small barn tucked next to the slope of the hill.

Penny the goat bleats at me the moment she sees the feed bucket. Her complaint is swift, nasal, and entirely ungrateful. I scratch between her ears anyway. She butts my hand in thanks—or demand. It's always hard to tell.

Our cow, Marigold, waits patiently beside the fence, big brown eyes tracking me. I press my forehead gently against hers for a heartbeat before filling her trough with grain. Her daughter, a mere two months old, joins in the breakfast feeding while I milk her mother.

The chickens scatter as I toss handfuls of feed across the yard. The rooster hops onto the stone wall and stares at me, head cocked like he knows something I don't. That wouldn't be surprising. I gather three eggs.

A breeze stirs the apple tree, shaking loose a few ripe fruits. I catch two before they hit the ground and pick a third from a low branch.

I return to the kitchen and put a kettle of water on the stove to heat. I slice the apples, toast some bread, and fry the eggs. Father trails in first, yawning, his hair in disarray. "Morning, Dess," he says, blinking blearily.

I hand him a piece of apple and pour water for tea, letting the warmth fog the edges of my doubt. "Sleep well?"

He groans. "Neck's got more knots than Calliope's yarn drawer. That'll teach me to fall asleep reading about Elarian linguistics."

"Did the great prince of vowels reveal his secrets at last?"

"No," he mutters around the apple, "but he made a compelling argument for comma placement."

Calliope enters a heartbeat later, hair twisted up with a quill stuck through the topknot. She wears a gown fit for a princess, but her yawn is anything but. Snatching a piece of toasted bread, she plops into a chair with the grace of a falling book. "Did I miss anything exciting?"

I set a cup of tea in front of her, along with a plate. "Only Penny's ongoing vendetta against the feed bucket."

"Tragic." She chews a bite of bread while seasoning her egg. "What's on the docket today?"

Father rubs his jaw, smiling a thank you when I hand him his breakfast. "A courier is stopping in this afternoon to pick up a scribed contract. Dessa, I'd like you to proofread it before he arrives. And tonight, the two of you are helping me translate an ancient Thornveil legend that arrived last week. The one with the triple curse."

Calliope perks up. "Oh! The one sealed in beeswax?"

He nods. "I'll need sharp eyes and sharper minds."

I hum my agreement and settle myself at the table. While Father and Calliope discuss the day's workload for the shop, I eat my egg and toast, but don't taste them. My mind keeps drifting to foreign kingdoms, scales, and broken sigils.

After breakfast, it's time to open the shop. Calliope unbolts the wooden door while I draw back the heavy, green curtain to let in the growing sunlight. Outside, the path is still damp with morning mist, the stones glistening as if kissed by ink.

Fable & Grim offers herbs, salves, potions, spices, and enchanted trinkets. Each item also represents a preserved piece of a fairy tale. When the book commands it, we hand out parchments containing quests for those who are worthy.

As we settle into our usual places—Calliope arranging the charm scrolls near the register, me straightening the shelves of storytelling charms and quill kits—she glances at me sideways. "Were you up late reading?"

I hesitate. She's always able to see through my lies, but I'm hesitant to share the details of the dream. Not until I know more about what it means, if anything. "A bit."

"You're bloodshot eyes tell another story, sister. Nightmares again?"

I make myself busy arranging bolts of cloth. "You worry too much."

"Then you slept well?"

She won't let it go. I move on to the rows of apothecary bottles, noting we need more bottles of pain elixir. "Well enough."

She doesn't press this time, probably because she senses I need to work through something. She continues organizing, but I sense her hurt at my reluctance to share. Guilt catches in my throat like a thorn, small and sharp.

Bells on the door chime as the first customers arrive. I greet a sleepy baker with a cough. Calliope helps an older man who wants willow bark for his joints. Then comes a girl who asks if our tea can make her dreams sweeter.

We do stock a blend for that very purpose. Perhaps I need some of it myself.

I restock the pine resin, check the candle supplies, and tell three separate people that *no*, dragon's blood isn't an actual dragon ingredient, it's a tree sap. A very useful one. Still, they buy more when they think it involves fangs and fire. The name causes my mind to wander, evoking memories of the prince once more.

*Drakenholt.* I'm sure I've heard it before. Seen it written down.

The most important customer arrives after lunch—a young man looking for a quiver of arrows. My sister and I feel it the moment he walks in, the tug of the quest.

While she and Father assist him with his purchase, I check the latest scrolls containing Vellicor's stories. "Wheaton Ysara?" I ask. "Is that your name?"

He's short and heavy and wheezes a bit through his mouth. "Yes."

I wrote his quest, imagining him to be...well, *more.* A dashing hero deserving of an adventure. I wish I understood what made him worthy of one, while I'm not, but I hand him the scroll. "This is for you."

His narrow eyes widen, and he wipes a bead of sweat off his cheek. "Is this...?"

I nod through my disappointment. "Looks like it's time for your quest."

Calliope claps once, triumphantly, and rifles through a basket of blank journals with dramatic scenes of heroes and heroines on the covers. "This one!" She whirls and stuffs it in his hands. "A quest journal. Every odyssey must have one."

Wheaton pales. "Odyssey? Quest? I just wanted a few arrows for hunting wild hogs."

Father claps him on the back. "The book has chosen you for this." He taps the rolled-up parchment. "It's your destiny, son."

Everyone in Evermere knows that you don't turn down destiny.

After Wheaton pays for his arrows and a few more items he decides might be necessary for his quest, he gives me one last fearful look before he leaves. I smile, trying to convey confidence that he can handle whatever comes his way.

He nods and walks out into the afternoon sun.

Refusing to let myself stew, I deep clean the rows of books for sale. I wait for the dream to fade, thinking my industriousness will push the memory away, but it does not. In fact, more images push forward. I sneak off to my room several times to log them in my journal.

Back out front, my head buzzes with so many questions, I can hardly focus on the gossip Calliope tells me during a brief respite late in the day. Something about a pirate who's come to town.

"I do hope he visits," she says, practically swooning. "I *love* pirates. They never wait for stories to choose them. They grab their stories by the tail and run with them."

My sister has always had the heart of an adventurer. I envy her that. Most of my life, I've been happy with a few good books and a quiet spot to read. My travels have never included actually stepping out of Fablehollow.

"I'm going to inventory the glass vials. We need more pain elixir." I slip past her and head for the back of the cottage. One of the many add-on rooms holds our supplies and inventory.

She doesn't even glance up from the romance novel she's pulled down from the shelf. "If you're going to the scriptorium, tell the book I need recommendations for pirate stories to read tonight."

I try to sound innocent. "Why would I go to the scriptorium for glass vials?"

She smirks. "The same reason you keep sneaking off to your room for crow feathers and ruby crystals?"

I shake my head in resignation. She knows what I'm up to. "There's something I need to check on. I won't be long."

"Go."

"I owe you."

She waves me off. "After dinner, you can tell me everything."

Maybe that's for the best. If I get the dream off my chest, perhaps its hold on me will loosen.

The scriptorium is silent and calm. The air is cool, and everything is in the same place it was this morning. I cross the worn wooden floor, past the desks of half-finished tales, to reach the shelves. My fingers scan title after title, parchment after parchment.

Nothing about Drakenholt is here. I was so sure...

*Vellicor.*

The owl watches, unblinking, as I approach. The sentient book still rests, its leather cover pulsing like a sleeping beast. Silver threads run along its spine, etched in symbols I've studied since I could read.

I place my hands on either side of the pedestal. "Once upon a story." I whisper the sacred words to wake it. "Tell me who he is. Tell me if this is my quest."

The book stirs, and a stalwart eye in the center pops open. The pupil gleams, amber and ancient, slitted like a predator's.

A dragon's eye.

I hold its stare as it meets my gaze. Gently, I stroke the spine and mutter enchantments it demands as a requirement to activate its magic.

Satisfied, it flips open the cover, and a wind that doesn't exist ruffles the pages. One page turns. Then another and another. Faster now. A flurry of movement. My pulse races. Then—

Stillness.

It stops on a blank page.

My stomach drops, my anticipation turning sour. No story is written here. No information.

*No quest.*

Something inside me buckles. I *knew* I wasn't meant for a story like this with a prince.

As I stare at the blank page with my heart in my throat and disappointment cramping my stomach, the center of the parchment begins to glow.

I gasp and step back. A word forms, burned into the paper, but not with fire. It burns with light. Lines sear across the page in glowing ink, curling and coiling until a single word appears:

*Longmere.*

I exhale slowly. A single word. Not a quest. Not a story.

A place.

The page cools. The burned name sets. And the scent of something familiar fills the air.

*Smoke.*

From the dream.

All of it comes rushing back to me. Not only the dream, but memories.

Drakenholt is real. The prince is real. Renwick Ravelle.

His parents, his baby brother...I remember them all.

And my mom speaking to the king. I remember that, too.

A creak comes from behind me. I whirl.

No one's there, but my pulse hammers. The book is silent again, closing itself. The owl blinks.

In the stillness, a whisper brushes the edge of my ear. "*He remembers you, too, Dessalyn Lorewyn.*"

# Chapter Three

## Renwick

I WAKE WITH HER name on my lips.

Not her full name—just the sound of her, half-swallowed by the dream. It hangs in my throat, raw and strange.

*Dessalyn.*

The hearth fire has long since gone cold. My cloak is pulled tight around me, but the chill has nothing to do with the air. It's in my marrow. It's the cold of absence. Of memory.

I sit up slowly, my shoulder aching from the way I collapsed against the outpost's stone wall sometime before dawn. I slept half curled against the wall and the loneliness. The journey here was never meant to bring comfort. It's a tomb now, like everything else in my kingdom. Stopping had been out of necessity rather than desire.

The ruins of the abandoned tavern groan around me, timbers long since split. Vines curl through cracked windows. Moss devours the walls where once the kingdom's banners flew. Drakenholt's colors, gold and iron red, have faded centuries too soon.

And still, the dream lingers.

It's been two nights, and I can't shake it.

She was there. I saw her.

Older, yes. Her cheekbones were sharper, more defined. Her porcelain skin was dotted with freckles. Her body, more curvaceous. But it was her. Same defiant fire in her eyes. Same way she walked, as if she didn't fully trust the world not to betray her. To shift under her feet without warning.

*Smart girl.*

She walked into the hall. *My* hall.

And I was on what's left of the throne.

I exhale, scrubbing my hands over my face, trying to smother the fragments of grief that come too easily these days. Since the dream, my mind won't stop circling around that moment, the look on her face. Her voice.

There was a time when I would have dismissed a dream like that. Called it the product of hunger and desperation. But that was before the forgetting. Before I watched my kingdom vanish brick by brick, name by name.

Before I forgot my own brother's face. My mother's laugh.

Now, even my own reflection feels like a stranger. Everyone I've ever cared about is gone.

I grip the shard of pendant dangling from my neck, the last piece of the royal crest that hasn't crumbled. My fist closes around it as guilt rises like bile.

This is my fault.

Because of Dessalyn and her mother.

Serenelle Lorewyn, the prophetess, stood in that very hall ten years ago and lit the match that turned the future to poison.

*Beware the crown that forgets its own story... A thief will come, not for your riches, but your remembrances. He will wipe your story from the realm.*

She'd said it softly, apologetically, as if the truth itself was a burden.

My father laughed. I did, too, behind my goblet. I was seventeen and drunk on power and court politics. I wore silks and thought my story too important to be unwritten. I was the heir of dragons. Untouchable. *Let the thief come*, I thought. *He'll have to get past me.*

Dessalyn had stood beside her mother, all elbows and sass, and pinned me with a scowl. She called me arrogant, nothing but a *stupid boy*, even though she was three years younger than I was. She taunted me, saying I was a boy who thought himself a king.

She wasn't wrong.

Pride and vanity had exploded inside me.

I didn't know then that Serenelle's prophecy would bloom like a poison seed. That the fear would curdle in my stomach and drive me to study the old magic beneath the library. That I'd break open the sealed scrolls, one I was warned never to touch.

Dessalyn's taunts and that vision became a challenge. A mission. To ensure nothing happened to my kingdom. My future throne. My home.

The nightmares began then. I didn't know my desperation to protect us would be the thing that destroyed us. Even as my parents refused to believe Serenelle's prophecy, it haunted me. I searched relentlessly for answers, options. Although I was training to be a great scribe amongst all of those in the kingdom, I didn't know yet how my powers might backfire. I tried to lock Drakenholt in place. Tried to preserve it in fire and ink and magic so old it didn't belong to men anymore. It was magic that could bend the bones of stories.

Stupid boy, indeed.

Stories don't like cages. When the Story Thief came, my words shattered. My family began to vanish, slowly at first, their memories escaping them one by one, until they didn't even know their names. Didn't recognize my face anymore.

And then they were gone.

I've been fighting him the only way I know how. I've written our history over and over, but the ink fades as fast as I conscript it. It's like trying to breathe underwater.

Only I remain. A failed prince and a ghost of a kingdom.

Until now.

Because Dessalyn came to me. Dream-walking through a kingdom everyone else has forgotten.

The girl who hated the palace during the days of her family's stay, while my father and hers created the great dragon library. The girl who scowled through every dance and called me broody and spoiled when she thought I was out of earshot. The girl who was exiled from our territory with her parents and younger sister on the night her mother spoke of the vision.

A full-grown woman now, she must possess her mother's gift. Even in her sleep, her presence burned. Her voice cracked through the fog of my grief.

If only I could have talked to her. Touched her.

She remembers. It's there, buried in her mind. Somehow, she remembers the place no one else does. Not her sister. Not her father. Not the maps.

If they did, they would have fixed this mess. Wouldn't they?

*Dessalyn remembers.* It's buried in her, tucked in the folds of dreams and stories. In her bloodline magic.

Her memory is dangerous. Precious.

A key.

I consider the possibilities. The choices I must make.

I'm the last royal. Perhaps the last person in my kingdom. Any day, I might vanish, too.

I rise, stretch the stiffness from my joints, and walk to the edge of the outpost's balcony. Below, the valley is veiled in morning fog.

Longmere lies beyond the curtain of trees. It's a place fraying at the edges.

I sensed the unraveling weeks ago. The signs are always the same—people forgetting names, histories, the shape of their own hands. It starts small, ends in ruin.

The Story Thief is circling, planning, ready to pull the next kingdom into the void.

And if my instincts are correct, that's where Dessalyn Lorewyn is headed. I don't need the Lorewyns' legendary Vellicor to tell me that. Or any vision. I feel it in my bones.

I curl my fingers into fists, fighting the whisper in my mind that sounds too much like hope. *She remembers.*

Not all of it. Not yet. But if she can hold onto the familiarity of Drakenholt a little longer...

I can use her to restore it.

She can save me. Save all of us from this brutal fading away into nonexistence.

But will she?

I drag my fingers over the dragon carved into my pendant, the same symbol that once marked the flags and banners that flew over every Drakenholt town. And then I pull my sleeve down to cover the matching tattoo branded into my wrist. Not to hide it, only to keep it from reminding me of what I've lost.

This broody, spoiled prince will do what must be done to bring Drakenholt back, even if it means trapping a storykeeper and bending her to my will.

Dessalyn Lorewyn remembers. That makes her the most powerful person in Edeia, and the most dangerous. I will use her if I must. Find her through the ink, bind her to it, if necessary. Rewrite the ending I couldn't save.

My only fear—the one that's closest at the edges of my mind—is this: will using her to save my kingdom make her a target for the Story Thief? Will saving myself mean destroying her?

I turn from the balcony. The road to Longmere is steep and treacherous. Shouldering my pack, I descend the stairs and walk out into the fog. I owe Dessalyn nothing, and she owes me everything.

It's time to go to Longmere. To her.

To a reckoning.

# CHAPTER FOUR
## DESSALYN

THE SCRIPTORIUM CANDLES FLICKER in their holders, wax bleeding down iron stems as the three of us gather around Vellicor's pedestal. Calliope perches on a stool to my right, her bare feet tucked under her skirt. Father leans against the desk on my left, arms folded, expression unreadable. I stand between them, heart pounding as I turn the book to the page that wasn't there yesterday.

"Longmere." I point to the scripted word. "It burned itself into the page after I activated the book."

Calliope squints. "That's not one of the marked story sites, is it?"

I touch the page, tracing the letters with the tip of my finger. "No, it isn't on any site list, but it should be. Something is wrong there. I think it's tied to my dream."

Father lets out a slow breath through his nose. "You mean the same dream you didn't mention to us this morning?"

I grimace. "I didn't want to burden you until I was sure."

"And now you are?" he asks.

I nod. "It was murky when I first woke, but throughout the day, I've recalled more of it. I was in Drakenholt. Or what was left of it. I walked through vast ruins and saw the prince on his father's throne—alone and surrounded by ash. No one else was there, only him. He was distraught. Smoke tainted the air. If I didn't know better, I'd say he burned the palace down himself, but why would he do such a thing?" They are both frowning at me as if I'm speaking an unknown language. I know my visions worry them, but they don't usually react like that. "He wore the pendant with the kingdom's sigil. And then this word appeared when I asked the book to show me my quest."

Calliope wrinkles her nose. "Drakenholt? Where is that?"

I raise a brow. "You know. The fifth kingdom of Edeia."

She gives me a confused look. "Did you hit your head in your sleep?"

"Of course not."

"There are only four kingdoms, Dess. Evermere, Thornveil, Aurelia, and Seabright."

I look to Father for backup.

His brows are squeezed together even more tightly. "Your dream has addled your brain, Dessalyn. There is no Drakenholt."

My stomach twists. "Yes, there is. I remember it, Father. Don't tell me my mind's broken just because yours forgot. I remember visiting it. Our whole family did." The memories are brief, but more and more are coming back to me. "I was fourteen and Calli was twelve. Mom was alive. You advised the king about his library. There was a feast, a dance—you wore that absurd orange coat. Mom spoke to their king. Warned him of something."

Father stiffens. He always does when we mention her. "You must be remembering a dream. None of that ever happened."

I frown, a desperate plea rising up in me. "It's not a dream. It was real."

He rubs his eyes. "Dessa, I don't know what's going on in that head of yours, but you're beginning to worry me. Your mother's dreams often felt real to her, too, but they weren't. They weren't real, and they weren't visions of the future. Or the past. Most were just dreams like we all have."

The floor tilts. I grip the desk to steady myself. Is he right? Is Mother's gift affecting my memories? "I don't understand."

He draws me away from the book. "I think I know what's happening. You want a quest so badly you're inventing one."

The words feel like a slap to my face, my heart. I'm speechless. I glance back at Vellicor, longing to touch the word again. Yearning to go to the town.

Calliope shifts. "Dessa—"

"No," I say, whirling on her. "Don't. Don't you dare patronize me. I didn't make this up. I didn't dream this into being. Something has happened to the kingdom of Drakenholt, and whatever it is, it's now happening in Longmere."

I draw away from Father and return to the pedestal. I press my fingers to the page again. The word pulses—faint, warm, alive. Like it's waiting. I don't know what I'll find there, but I know it's calling me. "I'm going to find out what."

Father glares at me, hands landing on his waist. "Don't be foolish. You're not going anywhere. Your place is here with us."

My father is a quiet, steady man. His quest happened when he was young. He got to be the hero, proved his worth, and ended up with a Fae bride. Since her death, he's lost his spirit. He only sees himself as a protector. Our guardian. I don't want to hurt him, but I'm not a girl any longer. "I love you, Father, but you don't get to decide my destiny."

His eyes harden, narrowing at the corners. It's rare I see such coldness in them. "You're my daughter. As long as you live under my roof, my word is king."

I step away and shake my head. I hate arguing, but I won't be swayed. "I'm also a Lorewyn. My story is mine to follow."

We stand there, glowering at each other. Calliope's eyes bounce between us. She's holding her breath, fearing what might happen next.

"Be careful, Dessalyn," Father says quietly. "You know what happens when we abuse the Lore Language."

A shiver travels up my spine. Mom's pendant heats on my collarbone. "Abuse it?" How could he accuse me of such a thing? The Lore Language is our ancient, sacred language of living narrative magic. It can bind, unbind, and alter the fabric of stories. Only those born of the Lorewyn bloodline can access it, and whether we speak it or write it, it always extracts a price if used for our own gain. It also listens, even when I don't speak it aloud. "I would never." *Not on purpose, anyway.*

"Of course not." Calliope jumps up from her stool and rubs my arm. "But you are obsessed with your quest. Maybe...yours is simply to stay here and hand out quests for others."

Another dagger that hits home. My chest contracts. Is she right?

I turn to the shelves, scanning the rows. "Fine. Let me prove it. Where are the records on Drakenholt?"

Calliope frowns. "Dessa, there aren't any."

"There were." I skim titles and juggle parchments. "I've read the legends. The dragon prince and his story-writing abilities. The great fire that birthed their dragon line of royals. It's all here."

Father walks to the map cabinet. He unrolls a large one and spreads it on his desk. His anger has abated to make way for logic. "Four kingdoms. See for yourself."

The map stares back at me, clean and empty of what I know should be there.

There is no Drakenholt. No royal empire or kingdom filled with cities.

My knees go soft, unsteady. "This doesn't make sense."

Calliope lays a hand on my arm again. "Maybe you're dreaming too deeply. Like Father said, the dreams are messing with your head."

I shake her off, hearing the whisper again. *He remembers you.* What would make us all forget an entire kingdom? I glance at my quill and the open ink jar. The unfinished story is waiting for me to resume it. "Or perhaps the prince's story is being erased."

Father rolls up the map and snaps it into a holder. "Enough, Dessa. You've been working too hard. You need a day off. I'll take your place in the shop tomorrow. You...get your head right. I'll fix you a draft to help you sleep tonight."

The worry in his tone trickles through my frustration. The anxiety in my sister's eyes makes me bite down on my next argument. I'm not winning this. They won't hear me. Not now. Not while they're afraid.

Fine. If they won't believe me, I'll let them think I've surrendered. It will buy me time to leave.

I pace the room, avoiding the desks and their uneasy gazes. I stop at my unfinished work and check the level of ink in the open bottle. Good thing it never dries out. I heave a tired sigh and rub my forehead. "You're right. The dream has messed with my memories. My mind is mixed up." I flip through the unfinished story. Stroke my quill. It quivers at my touch, ready and eager for me to take it up. I sink into the chair and dip it into the violet ink. "I'm not going anywhere. I need to finish this story. Could someone bring me tea?"

Father relaxes. Calliope looks relieved. Neither questions my sudden change of heart. My sister spins for the door. "Chamomile with a spoonful of my sweet dreams tonic, coming right up."

Father places a hand on my shoulder. "Having your mother's gift isn't easy. But sometimes a dream is just a dream, Dessa. Nothing more."

He eases into his chair and begins working on the contract he wants Calliope and me to review. As I reach inside me to call forth the Lore Language to finish the story before me, trusting it to feed me the words I need, I'm already calculating what to pack. How quietly I can slip out.

Later, once the cottage has gone still and their doors have shut, I move. I slip on my cloak and my boots. I gather a few clothes, provisions, ink, and my blade. I have no idea what I'm doing, but the first step is to get to Longmere. The pull inside me is too strong.

I take one last look around at my room and rub Mom's pendant between my fingers. *Watch over me.*

The back door always creaks, but I know how to muffle it. The humid night air rushes over me as I step into the garden.

A figure waits at the gate, hair wild in the moonlight.

Calliope.

She carries a pack of her own and has traded her dress for brown pants, a tunic, and a light jacket. "You're late," she says. "I thought you'd sneak out right after your tea."

I blink. "You knew?"

"Please. I'm your sister. Did you bring enough food?"

"Not for two."

She tosses an apple into the air, catches it, and takes a bite. "Got my own meals covered."

"What about father?"

A shrug. "Longmere isn't far. We can be there and back in a day. I left a note—sort of." She shrugs. "More like a riddle scrawled in his ledger. If he can't solve it, maybe he'll summon Aileen by accident. She'll be running the place before he can blink."

Our neighbor will be happy to be called into service, but Father will be furious. "You don't have to do this."

She presses something into my hand. A blank leather-bound journal. "For the quest." She smiles. "Let's go find this dragon prince."

I try not to smile, but something loosens in my chest.

We turn toward the misty road. Toward Longmere.

And walk into a story we're not supposed to remember.

# CHAPTER FIVE

## DESSALYN

QUEST JOURNAL, ENTRY ONE:

*Fairy tales begin with Once Upon A Time.*

*Quests begin with Once Upon A Destiny...*

*If this is the first page in a new story, I'm writing it in plain ink, not magical. No one, not even Father, can then accuse me of abusing The Language.*

*My legs ache from walking all night. The ink smudges with sweat and grime. But I write anyway.*

*Because the quest requires it, and this IS my quest.*

We walk all night until the horizon bleeds pink. Just when I start to wonder if I hallucinated the name in Vellicor, we stumble upon a farmer hauling apples to market. Roderic. Worn hat, wrinkled smile, no nonsense in his bones. He offers us a ride.

With him is a girl. She's perched on a crate across from us, back straight, hands folded in her lap. She seems carved from a storybook. Eleven, maybe twelve, her fancy dress is too elaborate for the road, hair curled just so, and her skin untouched by the sun.

"I'm Falena," she says a bit too brightly as we settle ourselves among the baskets. "That much I remember."

An odd introduction. Calliope sits beside me, admiring the girl's dress. "We're from Fablehollow. Where are you from?"

Falena's face pinches. "I don't... I'm not sure." Her forced laughter is brittle in the early morning air. "I'm having trouble, you see. I can't remember anything but my name. Not who my parents are. Not where I'm from. I just...ran. I know I ran." Her round, sky-blue eyes dart toward the passing tree line. "There was a man, and he grabbed me. He knocked me out, but when I awoke, I escaped. At least... I think that's what happened."

Calliope gasps. "A man kidnapped you? That's awful!" She goes to the girl and puts an arm around her thin shoulders. "I'm so glad you got away."

Falena nods. Her composure doesn't crack, but her hands twist together in her lap.

"Who was this man?" I ask.

Her expression sours. "I don't know. I can't remember that either."

Calliope pats her hands and brushes at a dirt stain on the girl's dress. "When he hit you on the head, it must have given you amnesia. I'm sure it's temporary."

Roderic glances back from his bench, the horse plodding along. "I don't know about that. She isn't the only one whose brain is woolly these days. Folks 'round here have been forgetting things for weeks now. Names. Birthdays. How to cook. Where they live. It ain't just the old ones, either."

Calliope frowns and shoots me a furtive glance. "How odd."

"A couple down by the river forgot they were married." Roderic chuckles. "Just woke up one day and thought they were roommates. Still argue like they've been together twenty years, though."

I tap my quill against my journal. More memory loss? "Have you ever heard of Drakenholt?" I ask him.

He squints at the reins. "Can't say I have. Is it in Edeia?"

Apparently not anymore. "We're searching for it. A place of shapeshifters and dragons."

He clucks at the horse and turns us onto another road. "Sorry. I don't think so."

I glance at Falena. "You either?"

She shakes her head, seeming frustrated that she can't make me happy by saying yes.

The cart rolls into town just as the sun clears the trees. Longmere is not what I expected. Familiar in shape—cobblestones and cottages—but strange in the way shadows linger where they shouldn't.

Banners hang across shopfronts in pastel stripes. Even at this early hour, children dart across cobblestones, squealing with excitement. A woman with a broom sweeps her front porch while whistling. Vendors call to each other as they set up their carts.

There's joy here. Noise. Light.

"Is this normal?" Calliope asks, shading her eyes.

Roderic grins, revealing a missing tooth. "The Queen is payin' us a visit. With her young'uns this time. Prince Morton and Princess Ravine. She was born here, y'know. Comes back every few years to honor the place. First time she's brought the wee ones, though."

Calliope squeals. Not just an excited gasp. An honest-to-ink squeal. "Queen Lavriel of Evermere was born *here*?"

Roderic laughs. "She grew up just over that hill. Family farm's gone now, but they keep the house as a museum."

Calliope clasps her hands together. "Do you think we'll get to see her?"

"Town square's the place to be. Parade at noon."

I jot a note in the journal. *The queen returns to Longmere every few years. This visit overlaps with present-day memory loss. Coincidence?*

It seems like a stretch, but I think of what I believe was the crown prince on his father's throne in my dream. What if the royals are where it starts?

Calliope chats with Falena about parties and palaces and dresses. We hop down from the cart when it stops at the center of town.

Falena hesitates, so I offer my hand. "You're welcome to come with us. I can't guarantee we can return your memories, but we'll certainly do what we can to get you home."

She flashes a relieved smile. Calliope and I help her to the ground. She's too composed for someone who's been kidnapped. Too polished. I don't trust her, yet I also feel drawn to her. To figure out her story. Even to help her.

If I have a guess, she fits the classic princess trope of those in Aurelia. Everyone is drawn to them. Everyone is compelled to help them and wants to make them happy.

Roderic tips his hat at us before he rattles off down the road, the horse's feet plodding away.

The town square is already filling. We speak to vendors and share our meager provisions with Falena for an impromptu breakfast. I have no idea where to go now that we're here. Through conversations with the vendors, we learn that the town has no library or bookstore, but there is a mercantile.

I lead us toward it, but my eye catches on a ruined church at the far end of the lane. Vines strangle its stone pillars. Half the roof is gone. But there are carvings above the door that have survived.

Something tugs at me. I cross the square without a word. When I reach the crumbling front steps, my breath catches.

They're crowns.

Four of them are still intact and easily visible. The fifth is a shadow—faded, weather-eaten, nothing more than a scar.

But it's proof. I gesture Calliope over. "Tell me you see it," I say.

She stares at the archway. "I... I think I do. There are five crowns."

My heart leaps. I'm not hallucinating. "It's real. The fifth kingdom. That's the crown of Drakenholt."

She angles closer, squinting. I see when the realization hits. "But if it's fading, and no one remembers the kingdom...?"

"Then someone's erasing it." I turn to her, chest tight. "I told you."

She doesn't argue. Not this time. Her eyes stay locked on the stone for a moment.

Falena steps past us and lifts the hem of her skirt to enter the interior. Calliope follows. I take out my journal and sketch the fifth crown in as much detail as I can.

"Dessa!" Calliope's voice calls from deep inside. "You should come see this."

I stumble over the ruins, and when I find them, Falena points to a long, stone wall with a mural, or what's left of one. It depicts a map of Edeia and...

The realm's *five* kingdoms.

Calliope runs a hand over Seabright and the faded monsters painted in the waters that border it. I touch the word Drakenholt, its flourishing script a work of art in itself. The artist has depicted dragons among its mountains and valleys.

Calliope turns to me. "So what now?"

I dust off an intact pew and open my journal. My quill and ink can't begin to do the mural justice, but I copy it anyway. Pressure builds in my fingers. If I don't get this down and quickly, it might be lost forever. "We find out who is erasing the memories of people and places and why."

As I sketch, the others wander away. "There's a small library," Calliope calls, her voice muffled. "But most of the books are gone."

A shadow flickers past the broken window to my right. I clutch my journal and shoot to my feet, the ink bottle shattering on the stone floor.

Heart pounding, I inch toward the partial wall on the far end of the nave, pretending to examine the painting of a saint.

*There.* Out of the corner of my eye, I see him.

A man in a dark cloak. Half-hidden. Watching me.

Is this the man who kidnapped Falena? Has he been following us?

My sister and our new friend are still exploring the other rooms. I reach under my cloak and draw out my blade. I don't know who he is, but I know the look of a hunter.

And we're not about to be his prey.

# CHAPTER SIX

## RENWICK

SHE SEES ME.

I should have waited and studied her longer, but the pull is unbearable. Every part of me, from human skin to dragon blood, drags me toward her. I'm about to step out of the shadows, slow and cautious, when she turns, sharp as a blade.

And she's already holding one.

Her arm is steady, stance wide, grip strong. She doesn't hesitate. "You've been following us."

I lift my hands, palms forward to show I mean no harm. It's not a lie. Not yet. "Yes."

Her voice cuts through the air, demanding, "Why?"

"I need your help."

She cocks her head. For a heartbeat, I wonder if she recognizes me under the hood. "Are you the man who kidnapped the girl? Hit her over the head?"

So she doesn't know me. She thinks I'm tied to the young princess. I am, but not in that way. "No, not me."

"Then why are you here?"

I could lie. Say I'm here for the Queen's parade. That I'm a wayfinder or a mercenary. "I believe my story is tied to hers."

The knife lowers a fraction. She narrows her eyes. "Who are you?"

A hundred answers flood my mind. None of them safe. None of them enough. "No one of importance."

Wrong answer. She steps closer, raising the blade high. "Try again."

It's humorous in some respects. I could overpower her with little effort. "Someone who knows what's happening here," I say, holding her stare. "To this town."

She hesitates and studies me. Her gaze is a fire on my skin. My cloak hides most of my face, but it doesn't hide my voice. Diamond pinpoints spark in her hazel eyes. Recognition? No, not quite.

Something else.

*Curiosity.*

She's trying to place me. Trying to decide whether I'm a threat or something more dangerous—an ally.

The blade lowers an inch.

"I know who you are," I say, stepping forward. "What you're able to do with stories."

Her eyes widen. The blade lowers some more. "Are you on a quest?"

Am I? "I'm not sure yet."

"Neither am I." Her voice hitches. "I mean, about being on a quest. I think I am, but..."

The moment stretches. We're breathing at the same time. In. Out. Pause. Something old and dangerous coils between us. Does she feel it?

Her eyes hold me like a sword to the gut—sharp, direct, unrelenting. She hasn't lowered the blade completely, but she hasn't run either. She's still listening. I could lie, or spin half-truths. I could walk away.

But I can't. Not if I have any hope of saving my kingdom.

Because she's standing here. Because she came. Because some impossible thread between us hasn't broken. Not after all these years. Not after everything the Thief has taken.

Maybe the dreams are doing what ink and blood and fire couldn't. Maybe she's the last piece of the story I failed to protect. Should protect now.

I take a slow breath. My voice is rough when it comes. "I need to tell you about—" The word scrapes my throat like broken glass. "About Drakenholt. About the—"

Pain detonates in every vertebra of my back. My throat locks. My lungs rebel. I choke on air, clawing at my neck.

"Hey!" She steps forward. "What's wrong?"

I drop to one knee, the pain blinding. The mark ignites, molten iron tunneling straight to my spine. I grit my teeth so hard it feels like they might crack.

"Say something!" she shouts.

But I can't. The Story Thief has silenced me. He's placed a muzzle on my name. My kingdom. My truth.

*Of course he has.* He couldn't erase me, so he bound me another way.

Dessalyn kneels beside me, her blade forgotten. Her hands hover—unsure if she should touch me. "How can I help?"

I shake my head. The only thing I can do.

Her brows pinch together. "Did someone do this to you?"

I want to answer. My mouth moves, but no sound escapes. The mark pulses again. My vision tunnels.

"Gods," she breathes. "You're cursed, aren't you?"

*Yes. And you're in danger if you stay.*

*Run.*

But the word won't come.

Footsteps pound in the distance. Shouting. Then a howl.

Her head jerks up. "What was that?"

Another howl. Closer. Followed by the snap of branches.

Her sister's voice echoes through the crumbling nave as she and the young girl emerge from whatever room they'd disappeared into. At the sight of me, they pull up short. Calliope grabs the girl's hand and shoves her behind her. "Dessa! Something's coming!"

I stagger to my feet. Pain still lances through my body, but I clamp down on it. "Go," I rasp. The word barely escapes.

Dessalyn glances around, swipes up her fallen blade, and plants her feet. "No."

Damn her stubbornness. "Go!" I shout, my voice stronger but still ragged.

Dark beasts appear in the doorway, the crumbled openings. Dark shapes spill through the broken archway—shadows with fangs. Wolves, at first glance. But wrong.

They're too large. Too silent. Their movements unnatural, as if some puppeteer jerks invisible strings. Smoke unravels from their limbs. Their eyes gleam like coals, red-hot and hollow.

My gut clenches.

*Storyspawn.*

I've seen their kind before. Felt their teeth and still bear the marks. They came for me in the final days of Drakenholt, when the walls cracked and the crown began to vanish. They are the Thief's hounds, stitched from stolen nightmares and spilled ink. Born from the bones of ruined stories.

And now they're here. He's found us. He must know she remembers.

I bare my teeth. My dragon roars behind my ribs.

Calliope screams as the beasts stalk us, focused on...

*Dessalyn.*

I grab her by the shoulders and send her sprawling toward her companions. "You must...flee...now!"

She whips back to glare at me. "I can't just leave you! They'll kill you."

The alpha licks his lips and bares his fangs at her. I lunge, grabbing my blade from its sheath on my waist, and attack. We roll over and over, his teeth snapping at my face, my neck. Dragon fire courses through me. I slice, stab, snarl. "Go!" My voice is a bellow now.

"Dess, come on!" my sister shouts.

Dessalyn, eyes wide in shock, hesitates only a second. As two more of the monsters creep toward her, she grabs her sister and Falena and shoves them toward a split in the far wall they can squeeze through.

She glances back.

Our eyes lock.

The world narrows to instinct and rage and the sacred duty of protecting her. With a quick movement, I slit the beast's neck.

The others charge after her, but they can't fit through the crack. She disappears, and fire builds in my throat as I throw off the now dead alpha.

I jump to my feet and shrug off my cloak. The other beasts focus on me. There are too many to fight with steel alone. They circle, abominations snarling with teeth made of ink and disease. The air thickens with their stink.

I can't save her if I die here.

So, I stop holding back. I let the fire come.

It starts in my core—a spark behind my heart, deep and ancient. It flares like lightning in my marrow, searing through my veins, turning muscle to molten steel and bone to embers. My skin stretches too tight over the beast. The monster. My back arches, ribs crack.

I welcome it.

Claws burst from my fingers, curved and obsidian-sharp. Wings tear through my shirt with a sound like splitting thunder. My boots split apart as my legs reshape, joints locking into something powerful and predatory. The shift is agony—but it's mine.

The change always costs me. The man burns away.

But she's worth it. *Saving her is worth it.*

The dragon rises.

The wolves freeze.

One snarls, backing up a step. Another whimpers—an unnatural sound from a creature that is more monster than I am. Their smoke-thin bodies shiver.

They know what I am.

And they fear it.

The closest lunges anyway—some blind compulsion driving it forward. I slam it to the ground, burn it. The rest scatter, slinking into cracks and ash and dark corners like cowards before flame.

Because even monsters remember what dragons are.

I throw back my head—and roar.

# CHAPTER SEVEN

## DESSALYN

WE RUN. CALLIOPE NEARLY lifts Falena over the ruins. I push on my sister's back, trying to make her go faster.

A roar splits the air—inhuman, full of fury. It vibrates in my chest like a second heartbeat. I spin around.

The church is burning. Flames erupt from the broken roof, licking toward the sky. Smoke rolls out in waves, thick and acrid. Something erupts through the rubble—massive, winged, terrible.

*An emerald-scaled dragon.*

Its wings slam the air. Its eyes burn with purpose. It launches itself into the wolves, claws rending, teeth snapping.

I can't move. Not due to fear. No, this is something else.

*Recognition.* Some part of me—older than logic, deeper than memory—recognizes dragons. *This* dragon.

My heart stutters. How can that be? Mesmerized, I take a step toward the flames—

The world goes sideways, a vision slamming into me. My body jerks without mercy and recoils, images overlaying the view in front of me.

Ash. Screams. Calliope bleeding. Falena gone.

*No!* I stagger back, gasping for breath.

Calliope's hand clamps around mine, dragging me back to the now. "We have to go!" she yells.

I blink and turn. And I run.

Because if I go back...I will lose everything.

# CHAPTER EIGHT

## DESSALYN

GRAVEL CRUNCHES UNDER OUR feet as the cottage comes into view. The night smells of jasmine. Tree frogs stop singing as we approach. Father's voice slams into us before we even reach the gate. "Where in all the sacred realms have you been?"

Calliope winces, shoulders curling inward. Falena stiffens beside me, clutching my cloak. I square my shoulders, boots dragging, the ash from the church still clinging to my skin. We caught another ride, but the last few miles have been all on foot. We're exhausted and limping.

He barrels down the stone path in his nightclothes, bare feet slapping the path, nightshirt twisted at one shoulder. His eyes are wild, hair tousled from sleep, or more likely, from raking his fingers through it in worry. "I wake to find you both gone and—" He pulls up short. "Who is this child?"

"We're fine." My voice comes out harsher than I intend, laced with the fear I refuse to examine too closely. My mind is swimming with everything that's happened, yet I can hardly speak simple words. "This is Falena. She's lost. Her memories of who she is and where she comes from have been damaged." I don't want to say *lost*. Not in front of her. She's fragile enough as it is. "I offered her a place to stay until she regains her memory."

He works his jaw. Starts to yell again. Then stops and shakes his head. "You *ran off in the middle of the night!* That is not fine."

Calliope steps forward. "We weren't in danger—"

"Weren't in danger?" His voice booms through the garden. "Two young women on their own, trekking through the kingdom, and you *weren't in danger*?" He gestures at Falena. "And then you dragged a child into it?"

Falena shrinks behind my cloak. Anger swims in my veins, even though I feel guilty for making him worry. I reach back, steadying the girl with a hand on her shoulder, and stand my ground. "We didn't drag her. We found her. And something *is* happening in Longmere. We saw it. Felt it."

He stares at me, breathing hard. "You disobeyed me."

Not for the first time. I see it in his eyes. I'm the quiet, steady daughter, but my rebellions have been a thorn in his side since I was a babe. "I followed the story."

He closes his eyes like that hurts more than any argument.

We file inside. The house exhales around us—familiar shadows curling along the walls, a kettle forgotten on the stove, the scent of parchment and old ink grounding me in memories.

"May I have some tea?" Falena asks barely above a whisper. "Please?"

Calliope puts an arm around her shoulders. "We'll make some together. Come with me."

I linger in the hallway, pulse still racing, ash still caught in my throat. Father's eyes are twin storms, relief and rage clashing just beneath the surface. I hand him my journal. "Your maps are wrong."

He frowns, flips through it, pausing on my drawings copied from the church. "You found this in Longmere?"

I nod. "Inside some church ruins." While the drawings are significant, all I can think about is the stranger. The wolves. The dragon. "The painting had five crowns. Not four. Five. Drakenholt's real. The map on that wall confirms it."

He reads silently for a moment. His jaw tightens. "And this man you mentioned—the one in the cloak?"

"I don't know who he was." My voice slips quieter. "But I think he's tied to Drakenholt. He knew something. He tried to tell me—then something stopped him. It was like he was choking on the words. I wanted to shake the truth out of him, but his throat was...locked, I think. His whole body shuddered like something was tearing him apart from the inside."

Father's brow furrows. "A curse?"

"Maybe." I swallow hard. "There's more. The church burned. Wolves—odd, monstrous things I've never seen before—attacked him. And then…there was a dragon. Smoke that choked the sky, fire that roared."

He goes utterly still, blinks, then runs a hand over his face. "But you weren't in danger."

His mocking tone makes the anger light again. The vision flashes in my mind. "We made it out safely." Thanks to the stranger. "And I know you think I've lost a cog up here"—I point to my temple—"but I know what I saw."

Calliope calls us to the kitchen. Steam rises from mismatched mugs. Falena clutches hers and refuses to look at my father.

"I didn't see a dragon," Calliope tells him. "Only those wolf-things. We were too busy running."

"I saw it." I press my fingers to my journal. "It looked right at me. Emerald green scales. Wings like thunder. It came from the fire."

Father paces. "You think this dragon was the stranger?"

My gut twists. "I don't know. But I left him behind, and I don't know if he's dead, or something worse."

The ache in my chest hasn't left since.

We gather around the table. I tell Father everything. Falena adds what little she can about what happened before she met us, her memory still riddled with holes. The kitchen fills with candlelight and quiet breathing and the rattle of teacups.

When the stories run out, Calliope grabs her satchel. "I took this," she says, pulling out a charred leather-bound journal. The scent of smoke wafts from it. "It was one of the few books left in the ruins."

The cover is half-melted, but the pages inside hold flickers of ink. I help her lay it flat. The script is delicate, almost ceremonial. She points to a half-burned passage. "Here."

We read together, whispering the words aloud:

"...the shadow-born sorcerer of Thornveil, cloaked in night, sought to bind the Lorekeepers. He envied their stories, craved their power. With silver flame and stolen ink, he began to erase their names..."

"Thornveil," I whisper, recoiling. "A sorcerer from the kingdom of shadows."

Falena lays her head down on the table, eyes lidded with exhaustion. "Dark, twisted tales and misunderstood villains." She shudders. "That I remember."

Calliope gently tugs the girl to her feet. "You're exhausted. Let's get you settled in a bed."

My sister takes the girl to the only spare room we have, while Father and I clean up the mugs. The cool water eases something inside me. When Calliope rejoins us, she looks as worn out as I feel. "She's sleeping already."

The three of us go to the scriptorium. Father pulls down scrolls and books, searching for information on Thornveil. We flip through them by lamplight, scanning for any mention of this sorcerer. Of shadow-born kings or memory theft.

There's nothing.

Was it always so, or has it been wiped clean?

Calliope's hands tremble as she closes the burned journal. "He wants to erase us so he can rewrite the stories and rule the realm."

"But how?" I ask. "Unless he's a Lorekeeper, too, how can he erase anything? Rewrite anything? He must be a sorcerer who was a scribe and is now using dark magic to do this."

At his desk, Father frowns. "The only way to erase us is through the stories."

Outside, a wind howls across the moor. Inside me, fear stirs. I can't let this happen. I won't. "How do we stop him?"

Neither my father nor my sister offers an answer. I rise, staring at Vellicor where it sits on its pedestal. The pages rustle like whispering voices. My breath turns shallow as one flips toward the center and stops. Words appear.

*He hunts the stories through you.*

I press my palm against the page. A single truth flares in my chest. *This is my quest.*

To save the stories.

The stranger was trying to warn me, and I have no idea if he's still alive. The thought haunts me. That I left him. That he may have burned.

But the story isn't done.

His.

Mine.

Ours.

In the dim light of the candle, I take up my quest journal and stare at the first lines I wrote yesterday. It seems like a lifetime ago.

*Fairy tales begin with Once Upon A Time.*

*Quests begin with Once Upon A Destiny...*

My destiny is tied to the prince. To dragons. To whoever is erasing the stories of our realm.

In the quiet space of my bedroom, I make notes, pages of ideas, theories, and plans. My quill flies over the parchment, the purple ink never dripping from my quill.

Sleep tugs at me, and takes me under at times. I jerk awake, scrawl more lines, nod off again. I write. Obsessively. Desperately. Like if I stop, the truth might slip away.

It's not the Lore Language coming through me. It's *my* language.

When I finally set down the quill and yawn, it startles me by lifting all on its own. It hovers over a blank page.

*What magic is this?*

The quill moves, and letters form words in a rakish script without the nib touching the parchment.

*Dessalyn...are you there?*

The quill nudges my hand, but I pull back. Then I blow out a troubled breath.

Finally, swallowing my fright, I accept the quill, dip it in ink, and write,

*Who are you?*

The quill hops from my hand and moves on its own again. *The man you met in Longmere.*

My pulse skips. *You're alive?*

*Do you remember me? From your dream?*

A dozen names flash through my mind. But only one fits.

I take a fresh quill and roll it between my fingers and thumb for a long moment, curiosity and foreboding tangling in my chest. I dip the nib into the ink and set it on the page. *Renwick Ravelle. The crown prince, yes?*

It's as if I can sense his relief. *You do remember.*

A smile breaks free from my lips. A dozen questions swirl in my mind. *What were you going to tell me at the church?*

*My story.* There's a pause. *But writing it out may be the only way I can.*

Because of the curse. I sit back and blow out a shaky breath. We are both scribes, the prince and I. Stories are the backbone of our lives.

Re-inking the quill, I lean forward once more.

*Please begin, Your Highness. I'm listening.*

*Dessalyn and Renwick have finally found a way to connect, but will Ren be able to share his tale before the Story Thief erases him forever? Don't miss The Flame and the Dragon, the next part of the quest in the Legends of the Five Crowns series.*

# NEXT IN THE SERIES
## THE FLAME AND THE DRAGON

*I'm the only one who remembers him—and the only one who can save him.*

In the realm of the Five Crowns, stories are power. Lose the story, and you lose the kingdom.

The Story Thief has already claimed Drakenholt, erasing its dragon prince, Renwick Ravelle, from every story in the land but mine. Now Ren is nothing but a ghost—desperate, dangerous, and determined to take back his crown.

I am Dessalyn Lorewyn, heir to a family of fae-born scriptographers who can shape fate with the ancient Lore Language. My duty is to guard the sentient book that records the realm's legends and gifts sacred quests to the worthy. I've waited years for mine...and now it has led me to ruins steeped in dragonfire—and to him.

Renwick claims I'm the only one who can restore his kingdom. But can I trust a man who might sacrifice me to save it? His touch is fire, his gaze burns, and the pull between us is a cursed magic neither of us understands.

Our journey will take us from enchanted ruins to the heart of Drakenholt's secrets. But when the magic we share comes at a deadly cost, I'll have to decide how much of my own story I'm willing to rewrite to save his.

*Slow-burn romance meets epic fantasy in a tale of found family, forbidden magic, and a love written in fire.*

# MEET MISTY

**USA TODAY Bestselling Author Misty Evans** is celebrating her 100th published novel in 2025. She loves writing urban fantasy, paranormal romance, and mystery/suspense. Under her pen name, Nyx Halliwell, she also writes supernatural cozy mysteries.

When not reading or writing (which is most of the time), she enjoys music, movies, and hanging out with her husband, twin sons, and three spoiled rescue dogs. She's a crafter at heart and has far too many projects to finish.

**Visit to check out her online store and sign up for her newsletter.**

*Read more at* _MistyEvansBooks.com_

# MEET MICHELLE

**Michelle Miles** believes every story should have a little magic, a dash of danger, and a whole lot of heart. She writes fantasy, paranormal, and young adult adventures filled with fierce heroines, unforgettable heroes, and the kind of romance that makes you believe in happily-ever-after. From angels and demons to dragons, elves, and time travelers, her books invite readers into worlds brimming with epic quests, high stakes, and enchanting possibilities.

When she's not crafting new adventures, Michelle lends her voice to other authors' worlds as a narrator and hosts *Miles Beyond the Page*, a podcast where writers share the triumphs and challenges of their creative journeys. A proud Texan, she loves getting lost in a good book, exploring hiking trails, watching her favorite movies, and savoring a glass of wine while dreaming up her next tale.

*Read more at MichelleMiles.net*

# ALSO BY MISTY EVANS

**PNR & UF by Misty Evans**
**www.mistyevansbooks.com**

**The Accidental Reaper Urban Fantasy Romance Series, available in ebook, print, and audio (through the Eleven-ReaderPublishing app)!**

Grim & Bare It, Book 1

Reaper's Keepers, Book 2

In Too Reap, Book 3

Killin' It (short story for newsletter subscribers only)

The Vampire's Kiss (an exclusive short story available in Misty's Store. Intended for matureaudiences 17+)

Grave Girl

Grave Magic

Grim Vows

Undead Ever After

**The Kali Sweet Urban Fantasy Series,**
**available in ebook, print, and audio (through the Eleven-**
**ReaderPublishing app)!**

Revenge Is Sweet, Kali Sweet Series, Book 1

Sweet Chaos, Kali Sweet Series, Book 2

Sweet Soldier, Kali Sweet Series, Book 3

Sweet Curse, Kali Sweet Series, Book 4

Sweet Malice, Kali Sweet Series, Book 5

Sweet Betrayal, Kali Sweet Series, Book 6

**Witches Anonymous Paranormal Romance Series**

Witches Anonymous, Step 1

Jingle Hells, WA Step 2

Wicked Souls, WA Step 3

Dark Moon Lilith, Witches Anonymous Step 4

Dancing With the Devil, Witches Anonymous Step 5

Devil's Due, Witches Anonymous Step 6

Dirty Deeds, Witches Anonymous Step 7

Wicked Wedding, Witches Anonymous Step 8

**Moonwater Paranormal Romance Series**

# ALSO BY MICHELLE MILES

**Age of Wizards (Epic Fantasy)**

In the Tower of the Wizard King

On the Hunt for the Wizard King

**Dragon Protectors (Paranormal Shifter Romance)**

Desiring the Dragon Lord

Seducing the Dragon Knight

Tempting Her Dragon Bodyguard

Dragon Protectors Book Collection (Books 1-3)

**Dream Walker (Urban Fantasy)**

Call of the Dark

Blood and Bone

Flame and Fury

Smoke and Ashes

Light of the World

Dream Walker Collection (Books 1-5)

Divine Heir: Dream Walker Origins

## Enchanted Realms (YA Fantasy Romance)

Once Upon a Midnight Clear (Cinderella)

Once Upon True Love's Kiss (Snow White)

Once Upon an Enchanted Kiss (Sleeping Beauty)

Once Upon an Enchanted Castle (Beauty and the Beast)

Once Upon a Midnight Dreary (Poe's The Raven)

## Enchanted Realms Related Novellas

Once Upon an Ancient Curse (Red Riding Hood)

Once Upon a Silver Strand (Rapunzel)

Once Upon a Woven Wish (Rumpelstiltskin)

## Five Towers (YA Fantasy Romance)

The Sorcerer's Daughter

## Highland Destiny (Paranormal Romance)

Desiring the Highland Laird

Loving the Highland Warrior (Dec 5, 2025)

Captivating the Highland Rogue (March 5, 2026)

## Legends of the Five Crowns
### *with Misty Evans*

The Lost Kingdom

The Flame and the Dragon (Coming Jan 2026)

**Ransom & Fortune Adventures**
**(Time Travel Action/Adventure)**
Highland Fling, Vol 1
Dead of Winter, Vol 2
The Citadel, Vol 3
Lord of the Underworld, Vol 4

**Realm of Honor (Fantasy Romance)**
One Knight Only
Only for a Knight
A Knight to Remember
A Knight Like No Other
Shadows of the Knight
Realm of Honor Collection (Books 1-5)

**Shorts and Anthologies (Fantasy/Paranormal)**
*Newsletter Subscribers Only*
A Dance Among the Faeries, A Short Story
Eorwulf, A Short Story
Dragons of Emhain Short Story Collection

*Watch for more at MichelleMiles.net*

www.ingramcontent.com/pod-product-compliance
Lightning Source LLC
Chambersburg PA
CBHW020333130626
46549CB00003B/1155